TITCHY WITCH

AND THE TEACHER-CHARMING SPELL

For Isabella
R.I.
For Matilda
K.M.

ORCHARD BOOKS
338 Euston Road
London NW1 3BH
Orchard Books Australia
Level 17/207 Kent Street, Sydney, NSW 2000

First published in Great Britain in 2013
First paperback publication 2014
ISBN 978 1 40830 714 4 (HB)
ISBN 978 1 40830 718 2 (PB)
Text © Rose Impey 2013 Illustrations © Katharine McEwen 2013
The rights of Rose Impey to be identified as the author and
Katharine McEwen to be identified as the illustrator of this Work
have been asserted by them in accordance with the
Copyright, Designs and Patents Act, 1988.
A CIP catalogue record for this book is available from the British Library

1 3 5 7 9 10 8 6 4 2 (HB)
1 3 5 7 9 10 8 6 4 2 (PB)
Printed in China

Orchard Books is a division of Hachette Children's Books, an Hachette UK company.
www.hachette.co.uk

TITCHY WITCH

AND THE TEACHER-CHARMING SPELL

BY ROSE IMPEY   ILLUSTRATED BY KATHARINE McEWEN

ORCHARD

Titchy-witch

Victor

Eric

Wendel

Weeny-witch

Witchy-witch

Cat-a-bogus

Titchy-witch *really* wanted to be
in the school play. They were doing
Peter Pan.

It was about a gang of pirates
who kidnapped children
and made them walk the plank.

Titchy-witch thought that being a
pirate sounded even more fun than
being a witch.

She tried all day to be on her
best behaviour so that
Miss Foulbreath would give
her a good part in the play.

But when Gobby-goblin started to
poke her with his poky little finger,
Titchy-witch couldn't help herself.

Gobby-goblin's finger grew and grew and grew!
Now she was in trouble again.

"What I need," Titchy-witch told
Dido, "is a teacher-charming spell."
Hmmm, thought the little dragon.
That sounded like a recipe for trouble.

But Titchy-witch's spell sounded like
a recipe for something much more
tasty:

Apples and chocolate and freshly baked cakes,
Poems and posies, whatever it takes,
To make the teacher forgive and forget,
All that I've done wrong and make me her pet!

The next day at school Titchy-witch's spell seemed to have worked very well. In fact, she couldn't do a thing wrong.

Miss Foulbreath called her a *dear child* and marked all her sums right, even the ones that weren't!

When the teacher gave out parts for the play, she told Titchy-witch she could play Wendy. "The *dear little girl* who gets kidnapped."

Deadlydoodle!

Titchy-witch wanted to be a *pirate!*
She didn't want to play Wendy.

But Primrose did. She told Titchy-witch, "I don't want to be your friend any more."

After that, things got even worse.
The teacher told Titchy-witch she
would have to wear a *wig*...

and *hold hands*
with Wilfy-wolf...

and *kiss* Clever Jack.

Double deadlydoodle!

For the rest of the day, Titchy-witch tried really hard to get *into* trouble and *out of* the play.

She knew that magic wasn't
allowed at school, so she gave
Clever Jack an elephant's trunk,

...and Primrose
a moustache,

...and Gobby-goblin
a giraffe's neck.

But Miss Foulbreath only smiled
and patted Titchy-witch on the head,
and told her how clever and funny
she was.

Titchy-witch was *desperate.*
She went straight home to make
another spell to put things back to
normal.

Stink bombs and fireworks and setting off bells,
Writing rude words and making up spells.
Talking in class and more petty crimes
To put me in Teacher's bad books this time.

Sure enough, the next day Titchy-
witch was right back in trouble.
Miss Foulbreath told her off for
every little thing she did.

In the end the teacher said,
"And as a punishment,
Titchy-witch will not play
Wendy – Primrose will."

Titchy-witch was glad to hear
that. She even helped Primrose fly
around the stage *without* wires.

"You're my best
friend again,"
Primrose told her.

Later, the teacher announced that
she had a special part for Titchy-
witch. But it still wasn't a pirate.

Titchy-witch stood in the wings
watching Primrose and Clever
Jack fly through the air.
The parents clapped and cheered.

Then she watched a little enviously
as the pirates fought with swords.
The parents clapped and cheered
again.

But the loudest clapping by far was
for the crocodile, who was
especially scary!

Titchy-witch thought that playing a
pirate would have been good...

...but getting to eat one was even better!

TITCHY WITCH

BY ROSE IMPEY   ILLUSTRATED BY KATHARINE McEWEN

Enjoy a little more magic with all the Titchy-witch tales:

Orchard Books are available from all good
bookshops, or can be ordered from our website:
www.orchardbooks.co.uk
or telephone 01235 827702, or fax 01235 827703.

Prices and availability are subject to change.